Praise for *The Naming of Tishkin Silk*

'This is a special, lyrical and lovely story. It gives you a vibrant sense of the Australian countryside, and even more, it takes you inside the mind of an ordinary but most extraordinary boy, Griffin Silk. It will surely touch your heart.' *Berlie Doherty*

'A poetic paean of hope, offering home and sanctuary to troubled souls of any age and any generation. This book nourishes the soul.' *Maurice Saxby*

'...a tender, poignant story filled with warm, wonderful characters and the joy of love and life. Filled with hope and compassion, this a delightful read.' *Sunday Tasmanian*

'...combines the themes of death, friendship, family, courage and the celebration of life... Glenda Millard's beautiful story will touch the hearts of all who read it, and will stay with them for a long time.' *Arrow Book Club, Scholastic teaching notes*

The Kingdom of Silk

Also by Glenda Millard

Layla
Queen of Hearts

LAYLA
Queen of Hearts

by Glenda Millard

Illustrated by Stephen Michael King

Layla Queen of Hearts

ISBN: 978-1-907912-25-2

First published in Australia in 2006 by ABC Books for the
Australian Broadcasting Corporation.

This edition published in the UK by Phoenix Yard Books Ltd, 2013.
Published by arrangement with Rights People, London.

Phoenix Yard Books
Phoenix Yard
65 King's Cross Road
London
WC1X 9LW
www.phoenixyardbooks.com

Text copyright © Glenda Millard, 2006
Illustrations copyright © Stephen Michael King, 2006

1 3 5 7 9 10 8 6 4 2

A CIP catalogue record for this book is available from the British Library
Printed in the UK

Contents

1. Blending In

Griffin came into the Silk family after Scarlet, Indigo, Violet, Amber and Saffron; and before Tishkin. And then came Layla. Griffin's daddy used to say that Layla had been sent to comfort them after Tishkin went away; like an arm about their shoulders, a candle in the dark or like golden syrup dumplings for the soul.

Layla had not been born a Silk, but her mother

9

said that she might as well have been. This made Layla wonder if a mistake had been made at the hospital where she was born. Had she been sent home with the wrong family? Was it possible that she was not an Elliott at all, but a Silk?

But when Layla asked her daddy for his opinion on the matter, he found some photographs of himself when he was a baby and some of Layla at the same age.

'There!' he said, smiling. 'Do these answer your question?'

In the photographs, Layla and her daddy could have been mistaken for identical twins, but not any more. Amongst other things, Mr Elliott had lost most of his hair, while Layla's had grown almost to her waist. But it made her feel special to know that they had started off looking the same.

'Then why did Mum say that I might as well have been born a Silk?' she asked.

'Well, you do spend a lot of time with them.'

'But Patrick spends a lot of time with his friends and Mum doesn't say that about him.'

'That's true. Perhaps it's because you sort of . . . blend in with the Silks,' suggested Mr Elliott.

'What do you mean?' Layla had asked him.

'Well . . . they're an uncommon sort of family. Some people don't feel comfortable with others who aren't just like themselves, but you seem to fit in as though you belong.'

Layla gazed out the classroom window remembering her daddy's words, and began to think about her friends the Silks. Besides Griffin, who was her best friend in the entire universe and was named after the mythical beast, there were the five Rainbow Girls, so called because they had all been named after colours. Then there was Annie, their mother, who wrote poetry and made the best bread Layla had ever tasted. Their daddy's name was Ben. Ben wore his hair long and he cried proper tears when he talked about his sixth little girl, Tishkin, who died before she had even been named. Ben could knit socks on four needles and carve beautiful things from

11

lumps of old wood. And then there was Nell, Griffin's grandma, who lived with them and who still liked to play dressing up and who had a tiny bit of magic in her.

The Silks didn't own a television. Instead they kept bees, a one-eyed crow named Zeus and a red dog named Blue, who was deaf but very smart.

Layla could see why some people might think the Silks were a bit uncommon, but she didn't see why that should make them feel uncomfortable.

When she had asked her daddy why this was so, he'd answered, 'I'm not sure, chicken.' Layla's daddy sometimes used the word *chicken* in place of ordinary words like *dear* or *darling* and when he did, she knew that a tender moment was coming on. So she had climbed up onto his lap to enjoy it. 'But I reckon there's got to be a philosophy behind it,' added Mr Elliott.

Layla liked it when her daddy was in a philosophical mood. It meant sitting in the old lounge chair that was nearly worn out, but that Mr Elliott refused to part with because it was just big enough for him and Layla to share.

Philosophising was a thing that couldn't be rushed. Sometimes Mr Elliott had to take a nap while he was thinking, which was probably why Mrs Elliott didn't bother with it, because she was always far too busy.

As the school day drew near its end, Layla remained lost in her thoughts. She must remember to ask her daddy, when she went home, if he had finally worked out why she blended in so well with the Silks when other people didn't. Perhaps she might find out for herself in the next two days. She had been invited to spend the weekend at Griffin's house, not that there was anything unusual about that, as her mother would say.

At last the bell played its end-of-the-day tune and Layla hurried towards the locker room.

'Wait for me, Griff!' she called as she grabbed her red parka from a coat hook.

'Why?' Griffin looked up absent-mindedly from his open lunch box. He'd forgotten to eat his sandwich again. 'Oh, yes! Now I remember!'

He jammed the lid on the plastic container and put it in his school bag.

It was about half an hour's walk from St Benedict's Primary School to the Kingdom of Silk. But when Layla went with Griffin it usually took almost twice as long, because there were so many distractions along the way. The first was Joe Canning's orchard.

'Do you think Mr Canning would mind if we had an apple?' asked Layla.

'Not if we take the windfalls. He doesn't sell them,' explained Griffin. 'He told Nell she could help herself to them.' He held the bottom strand of wire fence up while Layla squeezed underneath into the orchard.

Once inside, they chose an apple each and polished them on their sleeves. Then they lay back in the grass between the rows of trees, where ribbons of afternoon sun shone goldenly between the mottled grey trunks. Layla took a huge bite from the rosy cheek of her apple and sighed contentedly. It was Friday, Griffin was beside her and the Kingdom of Silk was almost in sight;

three very good reasons to be happy.

But then Griffin said, 'Did you get your report today?'

Before she could stop them, Layla's thoughts shifted to the pale blue folder in the side pocket of her school bag. In her experience, short comments, exclamation marks and silver stars were the usual rewards for good work. This report was crammed full of comma-studded sentences, unfamiliar words and strange, loopy writing.

'Uh-huh,' Layla answered through a mouthful of apple, hoping Griffin wouldn't ask her any more about it.

'Did yours have a note on the back?'

'What kind of note?' Layla asked.

'About Senior Citizens' Day,' said Griffin. 'Miss Beaumont talked to us about it. We're going to have a special day at school when everyone can take their grandma or grandpa along. Miss Beaumont said we're going to have morning tea with them and everything.'

'But what if you haven't got a nana or a pa?' asked Layla.

'Miss Beaumont said you can take anyone who's old,' said Griffin. 'That's why it's called Senior Citizens' Day. Haven't you got anyone to take?'

'No,' said Layla, and the word came out into the world small and lonely, like the sound of a pea dropping into an empty jam jar.

'We could share Nell,' suggested Griffin. 'She wouldn't mind.'

The sun was fast disappearing behind Joe Canning's apple-packing shed when Layla sighed, then picked up her backpack and squeezed under the fence after Griffin. If there was a way to measure love, she probably loved Nell almost as much as Griffin did. But still, she couldn't help wishing that she had someone of her very own to take to school.

2. Long Words & Lamingtons

As usual, Blue sat by the fence post at the bottom of the long, red-gravel driveway, awaiting Griffin's return. When he saw Layla walking beside his boy, he left his post and ran down the road to greet them. This girl knew exactly where he liked to be scratched. He groaned in ecstasy as Layla's fingers found that secret place behind his ears where his hair was still as soft as puppy fluff.

'He only ever leaves his post when you come, Layla,' said Griffin.

When she didn't answer, Griffin asked, 'What's the matter?'

At exactly that moment, Layla's heart was aching. Griffin's mention of Senior Citizens' Day had got her thinking about her nana. Almost a year had passed since Nana died and since then Layla had learnt to be brave, as her mother said she must. This seemed a strange thing to Layla and she wondered if her mother knew that although braveness stopped her tears from leaking out, on the inside she was still sad. In an odd way though, it was a lovely sort of sadness. It was as fragrant as the flowers in Nana's garden and as sweet as the last bite of a pink jelly-cake.

'Layla?' Griffin interrupted her thoughts.

'Oh, it's just my report card. It's got a lot of writing and big words on it,' she said, bravely ignoring her aching heart.

Blue sat on the road, watching the children's faces, disappointed that the scratching had stopped.

'But you're a good reader,' said Griffin.

'Oh, I can read the words. It's just . . . well,

sometimes it's a bit hard to figure out what they mean and whether they'll make my mother pleased with me or not.'

'Why don't you ask Nell?' suggested Griffin. 'She'll tell you.'

Oh, why hadn't she thought of that herself? wondered Layla. Nell had a special way of looking on the bright side of things. If there was anything at all good in that report, Nell would find it, and then Layla would be able to point it out to her mother.

Layla threw her arms around Blue's neck. He

could feel the happiness humming inside her. His tail thumped.

'C'mon, let's go,' said Griffin.

Blue stood up, shook a shower of tiny pebbles from his freckled coat and led the way home.

There wasn't a castle on the hill in the paddock that was the Kingdom of Silk, but there was a big old house with doors that were never locked, and windows that let the breezes in and the curtains out, and creaky verandas all around. And there was a red vinyl couch at the front of the house where you could sit and look down into the valley to the town of Cameron's Creek.

Nell was sitting on the couch wearing her cooking apron and a pleased look on her face. Zeus was perched on the handle of a garden fork amongst the weeds and marigolds.

'Hello, Nell!' said Layla.

'Hello, Layla. Hello, Griffin. Thank goodness, you've arrived in the nick of time!'

'Why, what's happened, Nell?' asked Griffin.

'I've just finished making a batch of lamingtons. I've been practising for Nina Corrie's funeral, and there's been no one I could try them out on. Chocolate's bad for dogs and crows, the girls haven't arrived home yet, and Ben and Annie are still mixing the bread dough for tomorrow and couldn't stop. Come down to the kitchen and we'll put them to the test.'

Layla and Griffin dropped their bags on the bottom step and followed Nell down the passageway and into the kitchen.

'Hello, Princess Layla!' called Griffin's daddy. He knew about Layla's fondness for daisy-chain crowns and still remembered the very first time he had seen Layla wearing one. She wasn't wearing one that day because the daisies only bloomed in spring, but it didn't matter because even real princesses don't wear their crowns all the time.

'Hello, Ben Silk!' cried Layla in return. Mrs Elliott would not have approved of her using Ben's first name. But in a quiet moment one day, he had confided in Layla that for his entire life, he had only ever thought of himself as Ben and that it seemed odd to him when people called him Mr Silk.

'Shall I call you Ben, then?' Layla had asked.

'Only if it feels right,' he'd answered.

Surprisingly, it did, but that was the way of things in the Kingdom of Silk. Things that would have seemed odd in other places seemed quite normal here.

Ben Silk held out his floury arms and wrapped Princess Layla up in his long baker's apron.

Then it was Beautiful Annie's turn. Layla always thought of Griffin's mother as Beautiful Annie, because she was. She took Layla's face between her hands and looked at her carefully. Not the way Mrs Elliott did when she was looking for bits of

breakfast that hadn't quite got washed off, but as though she was trying to look through Layla's eyes into her heart.

'It's good to see you, Layla,' she said, and Layla knew she really meant it.

'Oh, Layla, your face looks like a bap!' Griffin laughed at the floury imprints his mama had left on Layla's cheeks. Layla didn't mind. Baps, the large, soft bread rolls dusted with flour, were her favourites, and Annie always decorated one with a circlet of doughy daisies especially for her.

Though the kitchen table was enormous, it was almost covered with pieces of dough in various shapes; enough to make a week's worth of bread. Later on Nell would stoke up the wood stove and the dough would rise all night in the warmth of the kitchen. Then in the morning, Ben would cook it in the outdoor oven he had made from mud bricks.

Ben and Annie went to wash the flour off themselves and Nell cleared a space in the centre of the table; just enough for glasses of milk and cups of tea and a precarious pile of chocolate and coconut-coated cubes of cake — her famous funeral lamingtons.

'Help yourself to the milk and lamingtons,' said Nell. 'I'll make a pot of tea.'

'What happens at funerals, Griffin?' asked Layla, taking a cake. Although she knew that funerals were something to do with when a person had died, she wasn't exactly sure what went on there. 'And do they really have lamingtons?'

'It's when you have a sort of . . . going-away party for a person who has died, isn't it, Nell?' said Griffin.

Nell was at the stove, pouring boiling water onto the tea leaves in the pot.

'That's part of it,' she said, putting the lid on the teapot. Then she sat down with them. 'It's a time when friends and family can get together and share their feelings. There's the sadness of knowing that they're going to miss the person who has died, but there's also the happiness that comes from having known and loved that person.

'What about the lamingtons?' asked Layla,

wondering what they had to do with a person dying.

'Preparing food and sharing it is just another way of showing that you care about the person who has died . . . and especially about the sad and lonely ones who are left behind,' said Annie, who had come back to the kitchen. Then Ben came and they sat down and sipped their tea and tested the lamingtons. No one spoke for a mouthful or two and Griffin had time to think about what his mama had said.

'When Tishkin died,' he said, 'people brought us casseroles for dinner, and for ages afterwards Nell made us golden syrup dumplings. Remember, Nell? You used to say that it was good for your soul to make them and good for our souls to eat them, didn't you?'

Nell just nodded and clamped her mouth shut tight and Layla noticed that her chin was wobbling. She knew about the feeling that went with a wobbly chin. Carefully she licked each of her fingers. She could feel the thick, chocolatey icing sliding slowly down her insides and she was pretty sure that it was getting to her soul. She wasn't absolutely positive about what a soul was, but she imagined it looked something like a bird or a butterfly or even a kite, because Katie Wilson had told her that your soul flew away after you died. She sighed loudly.

'Oh, Nell, everyone at the funeral's going to love your lamingtons. Did Nina Corrie like them?'

'They were her favourites,' said Nell. 'That's why I'm making them.'

Afternoon tea at the Kingdom of Silk gave Layla the same feeling as philosophising with her daddy. You felt as though you could ask anything. So Layla pulled out her report card.

'I was wondering if one of you would mind reading this and telling me exactly what it means?' she asked. 'I think I ought to know in case Mum asks me questions about it.'

Nell scratched a dollop of icing from her spectacles and put them on. She read in silence for a while and Layla watched the expressions on her face, trying to guess what they meant.

'Unquenchable curiosity — that's marvellous, absolutely marvellous! Curiosity is a wonderful quality to possess; but *unquenchable* curiosity, now that's astonishing, that's what it is!'

'It is?' asked Layla, her eyes round with wonder.

'Oh, yes! It means that you never stop wanting to know about things,' said Ben. 'In my opinion, a teacher couldn't ask for more in a student than unquenchable curiosity! Don't you agree, Annie?'

Annie did. 'I do,' she said. 'It should be encouraged.'

'And what about determination?' asked Layla. 'Is that the same as stubborn? Mum says I'm as stubborn as a mule, but Daddy says that I'm only stubborn when it's absolutely necessary.'

'Determination ... mmm, I'd say determination is a smidgen different to stubborn,' said Annie. Mrs Silk was a woman who believed in the value of examples. 'Have you noticed when Blue has a bone, that he'll chew on it for hours until he gets to the middle where the marrow is?'

'Yes . . .' said Layla uncertainly. 'So you mean determination is in my bones?'

Beautiful Annie smiled and looked lovelier than ever.

'I suppose you could say that,' she said, 'but what I really meant is that determination is the not-giving-up part of a person.'

'Oh! Then it's a good thing. It's okay for me to be determined?'

'Of course it is, Layla! Most times, anyway.'

Once the unfamiliar words on her report had been clearly explained and the excellence of the funeral lamingtons had been established, Layla felt encouraged to tackle her other problem.

But first the afternoon tea dishes had to be dealt with. It was Layla's turn to wash. She put on Nell's long, green dishwashing gloves with the red fingernails painted on them. Nell believed in dressing for the occasion. But just as Layla plunged her gloved hands into the sudsy water, Zeus began to squawk loudly and flap his wings.

'He can hear the school bus,' said Griffin, putting his tea towel down. 'I'll let him out.'

The Rainbow Girls had arrived and, as usual, they would all be ravenous and very noisy. So

Layla knew that she would have to wait for a quiet interlude before she could talk to Griffin about finding someone special to take to Senior Citizens' Day.

3. Birds' Nests & Breakfast

In large families, quiet interludes are as rare as hen's teeth. They sometimes occur at the strangest times in the most unlikely places and must be taken advantage of immediately, before they are stolen away by someone else. It was almost unheard of to find one on a Friday evening in the Kingdom of Silk. But one was found, and it was Layla and

Griffin who found it. This is how it happened.

After dinner, preparations began for Saturday's breakfast. In the Kingdom of Silk, breakfast on Saturday was regarded as an OCCASION, with capital letters. Griffin had explained to Layla that when you said a word and then added the phrase 'in capital letters' it was like underlining something you had written on paper or saying a word in a very loud voice.

On this particular Saturday it was Griffin's turn to set the table; a task that was seen as an honour and required advance preparations. Secrecy was of utmost importance.

Layla felt Griffin take her hand and he led her to his bedroom. He shut the door behind them. Darkness and quiet closed around them as soft and silken as a cocoon.

'It's under the bed,' Griffin whispered and flicked his torch on.

'What is?' Layla whispered back.

'You'll see. Lie down on your stomach. I don't want to pull it out in case someone comes.'

Layla lay down beside Griffin. Somewhere on

the other side of the door, the floorboards creaked.

'Griffin, where are you?' The door handle rattled. The torchlight died. Layla and Griffin slithered quickly under the bed. A light clicked on, 'Griff?' and off again. The door shut and Layla breathed out in a rush of relief.

Griffin turned his torch on for the second time, pulled a shoebox towards them and took the lid off. It was full of tiny birds' nests. Wrens' nests and Silvereyes', woven from twigs and grasses, lined with moss and thistledown and bound together with strands of spiders' silk and horses' hair.

'Oh, Griff, are they real?' breathed Layla, gently touching one of them.

'Seven of them are,' he whispered. 'I've been saving them up for ages now. Sometimes after there's been a storm or when it's been really windy I find them on the ground. Nell said that the birds build new ones once that happens. But it takes a long time to get ten, so Nell helped me to make the extra ones. They're to put the eggs in.'

'Which eggs?'

'Ginger's eggs, goose eggs – you know,

tomorrow for breakfast.'

'Oh, Griff, what a great idea! They're so beautiful. You could never tell which ones you made and which ones the birds made.'

'Honest?'

'Cross my heart!' Then they heard Violet calling, still looking for Griffin.

'C'mon, we'll have to go,' whispered Griffin, as he put the lid back on the box. And Layla knew that this was the end of the quiet interlude that she and Griffin had found under his bed in the Kingdom of Silk on a Friday evening. She would have to be content to wait until the next day to make her plans.

When the weather was fine on Saturdays, the Silks ate breakfast outside. Ben was always the first to get up. He lit a fire in the dome-shaped outdoor oven to bake the bread dough that he and Annie had made the day before. The first batch was almost cooked when Layla and Griffin appeared around the corner of the house in pyjamas, gumboots and parkas.

The sun shone, the dewy ground glistened, and the aroma of baking bread filled the Kingdom of Silk. Nell was cooking pancakes on the barbecue hotplate and Annie was toasting leftover bits of last week's bread on a bed of coals. Blue was sitting very close beside her with a practised look of hope and good behaviour on his face.

'Happy Saturday, Nell and Annie and Ben!' called Layla, and if her words had been visible they would have sparkled.

'C'mon,' said Griffin, 'let's set the table before the girls get up.' Layla was carrying the box with the nests in it and Griffin had a large brown-paper bag. 'These are instead of place mats,' he said.

'Leaves! Oh, Griff, you are clever! This is going to be the best breakfast ever!'

'They're maple leaves,' said Griffin, placing one large leaf at each place around the long wooden table. 'Now we can put the nests down.' Together they arranged a nest in the centre of each of the leaves. 'I've got another surprise too,' said Griffin.

He turned to Nell, who was coming to the

table with the saucepan in her hand. 'Nell, can we . . . you know?'

'Yes, in a minute,' she said, 'but be careful, the eggs will be hot.'

Annie called out, 'Shall I wake the girls now?'

'Yes, please,' said Griffin. 'We're nearly ready.'

Carefully Nell spooned a boiled goose egg into each nest and then took something from her pocket. 'Here they are.'

'Look!' cried Griffin, holding out his hands. 'Nell's knitted beanies for the eggs.' Sure enough there were ten egg-sized striped hats, complete with pompoms, to keep the eggs warm. As she helped Griffin put the hats on, Layla noticed that the eggs had faces drawn on them. She could see at once that the faces belonged to the members of the Silk family. 'Who drew the faces?' she asked.

'Indigo, she's the best drawer. But I coloured them in,' answered Griffin, 'and Indigo let me use her good pencils. You know, the ones in the tin.'

Breakfast began when the Rainbow Girls arrived. Annie's bread made the best toast; crisp on the outside with a layer of softness, like the mist

that hung over the dam, sandwiched inside it. Nell cut the toast into fingers for dipping into the rich orange yolks of Ginger's eggs. There was a mountain of pancakes, so many that even Blue and Zeus were allowed one each, and steaming slices of oven-fresh bread drizzled with honey from Nell's bees.

'What are these for?' asked Layla, pointing to the small dishes piled high with broken chocolate.

'It's to make hot chocolate,' Griffin explained. 'You just put some chocolate in a mug and then pour in hot milk. But you've got to keep stirring all the time, so the chocolate melts properly.'

Breakfast took a long time, but no one seemed to mind. Nell looked up at the sun.

'It's almost midday,' she said.

'So it is,' said Ben. 'But making memories can't be hurried.'

This reminded Layla of her daddy and his philosophising, and she wondered if he and Griffin's daddy weren't so different after all.

4. A List of Likely Candidates

'What are you two going to do this afternoon?'
Nell asked Layla and Griffin as they carried the
empty dishes back to the house. Griffin shrugged
his shoulders and looked at Layla.

'I thought we might make a plan,' she said.

'What sort of a plan?' asked Nell.

'I need to find an old person to take to school.'

'Oh, you mean for Senior Citizens' Day?'

39

said Nell. 'I saw the note on the back of your report.'

'Yes,' said Layla.

'I told Layla you wouldn't mind if we shared you, Nell,' said Griffin.

'Of course I wouldn't mind,' said Nell. 'And I dare say there are probably lots of other people who'd like the opportunity to go with Layla, too.'

She set down a higgledy-piggledy stack of plates and saucers on the silver ripples at the end of the sink. Then she turned and looked past the bright braveness of Layla's eyes, to a place deep down where memories are kept. And when she had given Layla a thorough looking-at she said, 'But, on special occasions like this, it's nice to have someone special of your very own.'

'Yes, that's what I was thinking,' said Layla happily. 'I thought we could make a list and interview people.'

'That sounds like a good idea,' said Nell.

'What about Mr Jenkins?' suggested Griffin's daddy who had followed them into the house with a tray of hot bread. 'He's a nice old chap and I don't think he has any grandchildren.'

Scarlet was a keen list-maker and when she heard about Layla's idea she suggested a name.

'You could call it Layla's List of Likely Candidates,' she said.

'It does have a certain ring to it,' said Nell. Layla thought so too. Scarlet spelled the words and Layla wrote them down on a lovely clean sheet of paper that Indigo had torn out of her drawing book. Indigo had even let her choose a pencil from her tin box that had seventy-two colours, including seven shades of blue and five shades of green.

Layla looked at the gold writing on the pencils and chose one called Madder Lake because she liked the name. She had to concentrate very hard on keeping the letters from going uphill, because the paper had no lines on it. Then she wrote Mr Jenkins' name under the heading. While she and Griffin were trying to think of some other people to add to the list, Scarlet had another good idea.

'Why don't you make another list as well and call it The Main Contenders List?'

'What would I write on it?' asked Layla.

'Well, after you interview all the likely candidates you could write down the best ones.'

'What for?' asked Griffin.

'Layla might want to interview them again before she makes her final choice.'

'I'll write the heading if you like,' offered Indigo. 'And you can start on the interviews.'

'Okay,' said Layla. 'We can put some more names on the list later,' she said to Griffin, anxious to get started.

Mr Jenkins was the unofficial caretaker of the Cameron's Creek District Cemetery. He took pride in keeping the cemetery neat and was careful to preserve its calm and quiet atmosphere. The well-oiled lawnmower that he used once a week to trim the lawn section was almost as old as Mr Jenkins himself. It was operated by person-power. As Mr Jenkins trod purposefully and carefully between the graves in his crepe-soled trainers, its shining blades whirred quietly, tossing out snippets of grass like green confetti.

Blue went with Layla and Griffin. He was the only dog in Cameron's Creek to have Mr Jenkins' blessing to enter his cemetery. The first time Blue had gone with Layla and Griffin, Mr Jenkins refused to let him past the curly iron gates. Griffin had been about to walk all the way home again with Blue. But even then, before she knew she had it, Layla's determination had come to the rescue.

'But, Mr Jenkins,' she said, 'Blue's part of the family. He's walked all the way down from the

43

Kingdom of Silk to visit Tishkin's grave. He wouldn't have any wee left by now, and besides, he's very well mannered. He's not the sort of dog that goes around weeing on things of sentimental value.' Layla had no idea where she'd heard the phrase 'things of sentimental value', but when Mr Jenkins grudgingly agreed to let Blue into his cemetery, she guessed that she had used it in the proper way. To her relief, Blue behaved in a very dignified manner while she and Griffin watered the rose bush planted on Tishkin's grave and picked posies of yellow

daisies to put on graves that had no flowers. Blue and Mr Jenkins had since become firm friends.

But, when Layla, Griffin and Blue arrived on that particular Saturday, Mr Jenkins was nowhere to be seen.

'We'll just do a bit of tidying till he comes. Okay, Griff?'

'Okay,' Griffin answered. If Mr Jenkins was at home in his cottage beside the curly gates and granite piers, it wouldn't be long before he came out. His kitchen window overlooked the cemetery and nothing that happened within its grounds escaped him. He gave guided tours to strangers at short notice, whether or not they wanted one, and even tea and biscuits if they had travelled a long way. Nell said that this was on account of his loneliness. While they waited for Mr Jenkins, Layla and Griffin shared the plastic flowers from the graves that had plenty with those that had none. But when they had finished, Mr Jenkins still had not come.

'He might be sick,' said Layla. 'Let's knock on his door.'

45

But when they stopped outside the caretaker's cottage, Griffin said, 'Maybe we should just go on to the next person on your list. If he's sick he might be in bed.'

'But I haven't thought of anyone else yet,' said Layla.

Then the door of Mr Jenkins' house opened and a scowling, middle-aged man wearing a dirty blue tracksuit looked out.

'What do you two want?' he asked.

'We've come to see Mr Jenkins,' said Layla, poking her List of Likely Candidates towards him.

'What's this? I can't read it. I haven't got me glasses.'

'We want to interview him to see if he'd like to come to Seniors' Day at St Benedict's.'

'Well, he ain't here to ask and even if he was, he wouldn't be going nowhere,' said the man. 'He's in hospital. He's broke 'is leg.'

5. The Last Resort

Layla considered having something in common with Blue a huge compliment, but just how useful the never-give-up part of her would be, she was yet to learn. Without it she might never have met Miss Amelie. After all, Miss Amelie wasn't on the List of Likely Candidates, let alone on the Main Contenders List. So Layla could not have known that they would meet or that their relationship would outlast Senior Citizens' Day, or that it would become, what Nell called, an affair of the heart. It seemed that not even Nell had predicted this, because she had put Miss Amelie on a list of her own. A list she called her Last Resort List.

Nell didn't mention her Last Resort List until it was almost time for Layla to go home. Mr Jenkins' broken leg had been the first of many disappointments that weekend. By the time Sunday was over, the four names that Layla had listed as likely candidates all had lines drawn through them and there was nothing but the title on the page marked Main Contenders.

But even four disappointments were no match for Layla's determination. 'I'm not giving up until I find someone who'd like to come to school with me,' she said, and that was when Nell told them about her Last Resort List.

When Layla arrived home that evening, her mother was slicing vegetables for dinner.

'Hello, Layla,' she said. 'Did you have a good

time? Now, where's your report card? Patrick got his on Friday.' Sometimes Mrs Elliott forgot to leave a space for the answer after she asked a question. Layla took her report card out, but first she directed her mother's attention to the note about Senior Citizens' Day.

'I need to find an old person,' she said. Mrs Elliott looked at the note and then at the calendar near the telephone.

'You'll have to take your father if you want someone to go with you,' she said. 'It's the end of the month and I'll be far too busy at work to take that day off.'

Mr Elliott looked up from the newspaper he'd been reading. 'Senior? I'm not a senior yet, am I?' He ran his hand over what was left of his hair.

'I keep telling you to go and see the people at Hair Affair, Anthony. A transplant would take ten years off your looks.' Mrs Elliott tossed some beef strips and onion rings into the electric wok and turned her attention to Layla's report.

'But, Mum, I need a really old person,' explained Layla. 'Someone a bit like Nana would be nice.'

When a person has a mother who has an answer at the ready for any question, one who is never at a loss for words, an awkward silence is a thing to be noticed. Layla noticed. At first she thought it might have been because of the long words and loopy handwriting on her report, and prepared herself to do some explaining. Then she saw that her mother's eyes were very watery and guessed that it must be on account of the onion rings, because her mother was one of the bravest people in the universe. Layla knew this for a fact because she'd never, ever seen her cry.

'What about Griffin's grandma?' suggested Mr Elliott. He usually left these kinds of things to his wife to sort out, but he felt a bit uncomfortable about the awkward silence. 'I'm sure she wouldn't mind being a stand-in grandparent for the day and I know how much you like her.'

'Griffin's already offered to share Nell, Daddy, but . . .'

'Well, there you are, then. Problem solved,' said Mrs Elliott without looking up. But if she had looked up, she might have seen the signs of

50

determination that she was pretending to read about on Layla's report card.

'But, Mum, I want someone of my very own to take. Can I go with Nell tomorrow when she visits The Last Resort? Please, Mum, I've got to find a Main Contender!'

At last Mrs Elliott looked up from Layla's report and her voice was crisp around the edges like the beef strips that she'd left for slightly too long.

'What are you talking about, Layla? You can't just go off to some resort in the middle of term!'

Layla wished that her mother would come and sit with her in the philosophising chair. She found it much easier to explain things there. But Mrs Elliott was cooking dinner and reading her report, and the onions were making her eyes water. And Layla knew that it wasn't a good time to invite her to sit down, even if it was to explain about The Last Resort.

'But it's not far, Mum, just around in Chapel Street.'

'What is?'

'The Last Resort. Nell's going there tomorrow.

51

She said I could go with her if it was okay with you.'

Suddenly, Layla remembered the envelope that Nell had given her. 'Oh, I forgot, she wrote you a note about it.'

'Where are you and that sissy boyfriend of yours going?' asked Patrick the next morning. Mrs Elliott had told him that Layla was going somewhere with Nell and Griffin after school and that she wouldn't be home until later. Patrick was twelve. He had pimples on his face and the beginnings of a moustache, and he teased Layla all the time. Next year he would go to secondary school on the bus. Layla couldn't wait.

'It's a secret,' said Layla, with what she hoped was an air of great mystery. She threaded her arms through the straps of her school bag and opened the door. 'And Griffin is not a sissy!' she said as she slammed it behind her.

She was glad that her brother hadn't said anything about what she was wearing. Layla had

chosen her clothes carefully that morning. She
wore a dress. She had taken it out from where it
was folded in the bottom drawer and looked at it
for a while before she put it on. She remembered
everything about that dress. She held it to her
face and closed her eyes. It was old and washed
and worn. It was white with faded red hearts on
it. It had a frill around the bottom and a thin, red
velvet ribbon around the waist. She put it on and
stood in front of the mirror. The dress was too
short now, but that didn't matter. She knew that
her heart would never, ever grow out of it. Layla
put her arms out and slowly twirled, and the dress
floated like a dream around her.

Griffin noticed the dress. 'It's very pretty,' he said, and Layla let him touch the cloth and feel the velvet ribbon.

'My nana made it for me,' she said.

'I thought you didn't have a nana,' said Griffin.

'I used to have one,' said Layla, 'and she used to call me her Queen of Hearts.'

6. Plan B

Nell met Layla and Griffin on the corner of
Chapel Street with leftover lamingtons and an
armful of red and gold leaves.

'I thought we could all go together,' she said,
'then I can introduce you to Miss Amelie.'

'Miss Amelie? Is that the name of The Last
Resort?'

A chuckle escaped Nell. 'I suppose you could

say that. Yes, Miss Amelie is the person we're going to visit.'

'Mum didn't understand about The Last Resort,' said Layla. 'She thought it was some place where you go for a holiday.'

'Oh dear,' said Nell.

'It's like plan B,' said Griffin.

'I know that,' said Layla. 'Nell told me that a last resort is something you try when all else has failed. But it was hard to explain to Mum. Then I remembered Nell's note and everything was okay.'

'I'm glad about that,' said Nell.

'Me too,' said Layla. 'I can't wait to meet Miss Amelie.' She skipped along in the gutter for a while, rustling the fallen leaves with her trainers, then she asked, 'Nell, why didn't we put Miss Amelie on the List of Likely Candidates?'

'Because I'm not quite sure if she is a likely candidate.'

'Why not?' asked Griffin.

'Well, she's a bit forgetful and she gets muddled at new things or different places and people. So she doesn't go out much. That's why I visit her.

But I thought that if you came with me each time I visited, she'd probably get used to you and she might even be persuaded to go to school with you on Senior Citizens' Day.'

'And you'll be there, too,' said Layla, tossing a handful of yellow leaves into the air, 'and you make people feel not afraid of anything.'

Nell squeezed Layla's hand tight. 'We'll have to see what happens,' she said.

Miss Amelie was tall and thin, with straight, short, silver hair; not at all what Layla had expected. Not a bit like Nana had been. Miss Amelie wore neat tartan trousers, a black sweater and sensible lace-up walking shoes. Her shoulders were slightly stooped and her head drooped shyly, the way a violet's does.

When Nell introduced Layla, Miss Amelie knitted her brows together and stared at Layla's face, as though she was trying to remember something.

'Do I know you?' she asked.

'No, not yet,' said Layla. Then she slipped her hand into Miss Amelie's and squeezed it the way Nell had squeezed hers. 'But don't worry, Miss Amelie, you soon will.'

Griffin was watching. He remembered the day he'd started school; when some of the big boys had been teasing him. Despite being smaller than he was, Layla had come to his rescue. Something told him that Layla was planning to rescue Miss

Amelie too, although he couldn't have said what it was that she needed rescuing from.

'And this is my grandson, Griffin, Amelie,' said Nell. Gravely, Griffin offered his hand.

'I'm pleased to meet you, Miss Amelie.'

'Griffin,' she said and the worried look came back. She went to a drawer near the sink and came back with a used envelope and a pencil. 'Write it down,' she said, handing them to Griffin.

'What do you want me to write?' asked Griffin.

'The thing you told me,' said Miss Amelie.

'Your names, Griffin,' said Nell, 'yours and Layla's, so that Miss Amelie can remember them.'

'Yes,' said Miss Amelie, nodding, 'write your names.'

Nell put the lamingtons on a plate and the leaves in a tall china vase and water in the kettle to make tea. Miss Amelie didn't seem to mind at all, even though it was her house, not Nell's.

Griffin wrote Layla's name and then his own in large clear letters on the envelope. He showed them to Miss Amelie, who read them out loud and looked very pleased. Then she fixed the envelope to the refrigerator with a magnet, beside the many other notes that were there.

'Layla and Griffin,' she said. 'Griffin. I have a book about griffins.'

'So has my daddy,' said Griffin. 'It's got lots of other mythical beasts in it too.'

'Ah, myths and legends, beasts and books!' said Miss Amelie, and Layla heard a sparkle in her voice and saw a spring in her step as she crossed the room and opened the door. Shelves of books covered two walls of Miss Amelie's sitting room, from floor to ceiling. But amongst the hundreds of books, Miss Amelie knew exactly where to find the one about griffins. It was large and heavy with golden edges to its pages and a narrow blue ribbon with a tassel to mark items of interest. It was called *Griffins and Gargoyles in Architecture*. Miss Amelie put it on the table. 'There,' she said, 'a whole book about griffins!' She seemed very pleased about her book of griffins.

She sat between Layla and Griffin and began to turn the glossy pages. On each of them were photographs of griffins: carved wooden griffins,

marble griffins, bronze griffins and stone griffins. There were griffins on churches, on museums and in galleries. Miss Amelie had seen them all. She remembered in which year she had seen each one, in which month of that year and in which city. 'In Vienna,' she'd say, or, 'in Rome. It was August and we ate vanilla ice-cream that day.' She could even remember the weather. 'It rained steadily in Paris on the day I first saw Notre Dame.'

While Miss Amelie talked and turned the pages of her life, Layla went with her to the faraway places, shared the sights, the sounds and the scents. The feeling that came over her was almost the same as when she sat with her daddy on the philosophising chair or when she took afternoon tea in the Kingdom of Silk. And, like her daddy and the Silks, Miss Amelie didn't seem to mind that Layla's curiosity was unquenchable. She answered every question politely and as patiently as though it was the very first one.

So when Nell said that it was time to go, Layla was surprised and disappointed. And so, it seemed, was Miss Amelie.

'So soon?' she said. 'Will you come again?'

'Of course, Amelie,' said Nell.

'And the children?'

'Would you like them to?'

'Yes, I want them to come back,' said Miss Amelie, wringing her hands together. 'People say they'll come back, but they never do.'

'We will, Miss Amelie,' said Layla, 'cross my heart.' But Miss Amelie's hands were still restless and Layla could see that she needed reassurance. So although it was only her very first visit, Layla said, 'I'm going to put you right on top of my Main Contenders List, Miss Amelie.' Miss Amelie was completely speechless then and Layla supposed that it was because she was so surprised.

As they walked towards Layla's house, Nell said, 'Layla, I want you to remember that even though you might like Miss Amelie very much, it will still be up to her whether or not she comes to Senior Citizens' Day. There's also a possibility that even if she does agree, she might forget about it. That's why she wasn't on your List of Likely Candidates.'

'Yes, I know,' said Layla.

'It's just that I don't want you to be disappointed. Now, you're sure you want to come with me again on Wednesday?'

'Wednesday? Couldn't we go tomorrow?' asked Layla. 'Miss Amelie might think we're not coming back if we don't go tomorrow. Couldn't Griffin and I go by ourselves? Please, Nell?'

'I'm not sure that would be a good idea,' said

Nell. 'It takes her a while to get used to different people and things. She might get in a dither if you arrive by yourselves and she can't remember who you are.'

'But I wrote our names down for her,' said Griffin. 'And she remembered all about the griffins she saw a long time ago.'

'Yes,' said Nell, 'but Miss Amelie can remember things from a long time ago much better than things that have just happened. When I first began to visit her, she'd forget, every time, that we'd met before. But rather than upset her by telling her that she already knew me, I'd just behave as though it was the first time I'd been there and introduce myself all over again. Even now, sometimes it takes her a moment or two to remember. So I think it would be best if we all went together again on Wednesday. If she sees me with you, she's more likely to remember that she's met you before.'

Layla made up her mind right then that if Nell had been prepared to make-believe for Miss Amelie's sake, then so would she. But already there was a little ache inside her that wanted Miss Amelie to remember her and it was separate from the part of her that wanted Miss Amelie to be a Likely Candidate.

7. Consequences

One of Mr Elliott's favourite sayings was 'for every action there is a consequence'. He said it was one of the rules of life and that it was important everyone knew about it. Layla often heard him quoting this rule to Patrick, although Patrick never seemed very interested that the things he did caused other things to happen. Layla, on the other hand, was very interested, for on many occasions a consequence cannot be known or even guessed at. Layla's gift of two photographs to Miss Amelie was an action where the final consequence was to be one of great mystery.

The idea about the photographs didn't come to Layla until she and Griffin had visited Miss Amelie several times. On each of these occasions they had to remind her who they were and to pretend for her sake, just as Nell had, that this was their first visit. As soon as Griffin's name was mentioned, Layla imagined a bell going 'ding' inside Miss Amelie's head as she remembered her book with the gilt-edged pages, *Griffins and Gargoyles in Architecture*. Then, just like clockwork, she'd hurry across and take it down from the shelves.

'There,' she'd say, 'a whole book about griffins!' And only then, when everything seemed to be exactly as it had been the time before, was Miss Amelie content.

This led Layla in search of other ways that

might help Miss Amelie remember. The next time Miss Amelie opened her door, she looked straight at the bold writing on the sticky labels on the chests of Layla and Griffin. She read out their names, twice over.

'Layla, Griffin. Layla and Griffin.' Then, after a short space left for thinking, Miss Amelie looked at Nell and said, 'You've brought Layla and Griffin, Nell!'

And Nell said, 'Yes, Amelie,' in such an ordinary, everyday sort of voice that no one, except for Layla and Griffin, would have known that this was a significant moment. It was such a significant moment that Layla's journal entry the following day at school read: *Miss Amelie remembered me and Griffin all by herself and it was because of the sticky notes.*

Layla began to visit Miss Amelie every day after school from then on, usually with Nell and Griffin, but sometimes just she and Griffin went. Most days Miss Amelie remembered right away who they were, but there were still a few occasions when it took a little longer. Those few occasions were the reason that Layla had brought the photographs of unknown consequence with her; one of herself and one of Griffin. She had glued them to pieces of white cardboard and written their names under them. These photographs led to Layla discovering much about Miss Amelie and a little about someone called John William.

It was the first time she had visited Miss Amelie all by herself.

When Layla gave her the photographs, Miss Amelie said, 'For me?' Layla could tell by the sound of her voice and the way her eyebrows shot up under her silver fringe that she was pleasantly surprised.

'Yes, you can keep them,' said Layla.

'I have many photographs,' said Miss Amelie, 'but none like these.' She leaned them against the vase that held the autumn leaves that Nell had brought down from the Kingdom of Silk. Miss Amelie didn't sweep the fallen ones into the rubbish like Mrs Elliott would have. She left them on the table where they looked every bit as beautiful as they had done in the vase.

'Can we look at your photographs, Miss Amelie?' asked Layla. Miss Amelie's photographs were as neat as she was. They were kept in albums, held in place with tiny golden triangles on chocolate-brown pages and separated by sheets of almost-transparent tissue paper. Through the tissue, the old photographs looked like dreams.

Layla took her shoes off, so that she could sit up on the sofa with Miss Amelie and look at the photographs. At first Miss Amelie was distracted by Layla's toenails. She told Layla that she had never seen toenails painted pink with red hearts. She couldn't stop looking at them and Layla could tell that she was impressed.

'You just paint them and stick the hearts on when they're dry,' she explained. 'I could do yours, if you like. Nell lets me paint hers sometimes when her corns aren't playing up and sometimes, when the Rainbow Girls aren't home, Griffin lets me do his.' When Miss Amelie didn't answer, Layla added, 'I've got other stickers. If you don't like hearts you

could have stars.' Still Miss Amelie didn't say a word
and Layla thought that she might have muddled
her a bit, and she didn't want that to happen. But
as it turned out, Miss Amelie wasn't muddled at all;
she had just been thinking.

'I do like hearts,' she said, 'like the ones on your
dress, your Queen of Hearts dress.'

Layla was not prepared for another significant
moment so soon after the last one, especially one
as astonishing as this. How could Miss Amelie
have known that this was what Nana had called
the dress?

'How did you know?' she asked, but Miss
Amelie's thoughts had taken her to somewhere else.

'That's what John William calls me,' she said,
'his Queen of Hearts.'

'Who is John William?' asked Layla.

'I'll find a picture of him,' Miss Amelie said. But
there were many albums and many photographs;
photographs of long ago when Miss Amelie was
a baby, and of later on when she was a young
woman, a school teacher, when her shoulders
had been straight, not stooped, and her hair was

long and dark like Layla's. And when it was time for Layla to go home, still John William had not been found. But Layla would learn that although Miss Amelie sometimes got muddled, there were some things she never forgot. John William was one of them.

'Goodbye, Layla,' she said. 'I'll look for John William while you're away.'

When Layla went back to Miss Amelie's it was Friday and there were only five days left before Seniors' Day. Miss Amelie was waiting at her gate. Layla and Griffin could see her from the corner. It was the first time they had seen Miss Amelie outside. They waved to her, but she didn't wave back and Layla had the feeling that something was not quite right.

'C'mon, Griff, let's run,' she said.

'Have you seen my John William?' asked Miss Amelie when they arrived. But she wasn't looking at them. Her eyes were staring down the road into the distance.

'No,' said Layla. 'You were going to find a picture of him for me. Don't you remember?'

'I thought you might have seen him on the way here,' said Miss Amelie.

'What does he look like?' asked Griffin.

'He's a tall and handsome young man,' she said.

Layla couldn't think of any tall and handsome young men they'd seen that day.

'Oh dear,' said Miss Amelie, 'I felt sure that he would come today.'

'Has he been here before?' asked Layla, wondering if Miss Amelie's visitor had lost his way.

'Oh yes, John William was born in Cameron's Creek.'

'Then maybe he'll come later,' said Layla. 'How is he getting here?'

'He went away on the train,' said Miss Amelie.

'Will he come back on the train too?' asked Layla.

'I suppose so.'

'Well, that's okay then,' said Layla. 'John William won't be home till later. The train hasn't come yet.'

'Later . . . He'll come later?'

'Yes, it's too early for the train. Can we go inside now, Miss Amelie? You could show us John William's picture and then Griffin and I will know who he is when he comes.'

At last Miss Amelie was persuaded to go into her house, where a photograph album lay open on the kitchen table.

'Look, there he is. There's John William and me,' said Miss Amelie. Layla and Griffin looked where Miss Amelie was pointing.

'Who is John William?' asked Griffin.

'John William is my beau,' answered Miss Amelie, and her violet head tilted to one side the way the head sometimes will when a secret escapes the heart.

'What's a beau?' asked Layla.

'A sweetheart,' said Miss Amelie. The photograph was of a young man in a soldier's uniform, standing arm in arm with Miss Amelie, who was also young and straight and tall. The photograph had been taken a very long time ago. The feeling that something wasn't quite right came back and suddenly Layla wished that Nell wasn't getting her corns seen to.

But Nell wasn't there and there were only four more sleeps until it was Senior Citizens' Day. And Layla still hadn't asked Miss Amelie if she would come to St Benedict's with her. She didn't want anything to stop Miss Amelie from coming, not even John William. So although she had promised Nell that she wouldn't, the feeling that something was not quite right made Layla ask, 'Miss Amelie, will you come to school with me?'

'I must be here when John William comes,' she answered. 'I told him that I'd wait for him.'

'Not today, school's finished today,' said Layla.

To Layla's surprise, Miss Amelie didn't seem at all muddled and agreed at once.

'Oh, another day. Yes, I'll come another day,' she said. Layla smiled happily at Griffin, but then Miss Amelie added, 'After John William comes home.'

8. The Soldier Boy

According to Nell, Sunday was a day of rest, especially if you'd just had your corns done. She was sitting on the back veranda with Layla and Griffin looking down past the dam where Ben and Annie were picking the last of the season's grapes. The sun was low, the water gleamed, and leafless vines scribbled secret words along the wires. The kitchen was full of Rainbow Girls and tantalising aromas. Layla had persuaded Nell to take her feet out of her lambswool slippers and to prop them on a squat, velvet-covered stool so that she could inspect them at close quarters. There were patches of sticking plaster on the toes where the hard lumps had once been. Layla noticed that not only the corns were gone, but also most of the nail polish that she had painted on. Only the hearts were still there.

'I might do Miss Amelie's toenails before she comes to Seniors' Day.' Layla's thoughts became words before she could stop them.

'So you've already invited her?' asked Nell, and Layla bit her lip and nodded.

'There's only two sleeps to go now,' she explained and then said reassuringly, 'and she didn't seem a bit muddled.'

'And she's agreed to go with you?' Layla nodded again and Nell said, 'Marvellous!' Then after a pause she added, 'But I think we'll call in tomorrow, just to remind her.'

'But what about your feet, Nell?'

'I'm sure they'll be much better by then,'

said Nell, 'and if not, I'll just have to wear my slippers.'

Layla was pleased. Nell was a person you could rely on to sort everything out, but she began to wonder if she should mention Miss Amelie's beau and the photograph. Then the Rainbow Girls arrived with a very late afternoon tea.

'Corns or no corns, there's always something to be thankful for!' said Nell as Amber carefully balanced a tea tray on her lap. That put an end to Layla's wondering and the feeling that something was not quite right, at least for the time being. She leaned her back against the veranda post. Nell was right. There was a baby's bath full of sweet black grapes, a fat orange sun floating in the dam, a magpie choir, the smell of woodsmoke, upside-down apple cake and tea.

When it was time for Layla to go home, Nell put her feet back in her slippers and stood up.

'It's okay, Nell. I'll walk Layla down to Canning's dam,' said Griffin.

But Nell had a knack for knowing when a girl wanted to get something off her chest. She said, 'I need to get in some practice before tomorrow, but I'll only come down as far as the gate.' This was the opportunity that Layla had been waiting for; the chance to bring up the matter of John William. It was lucky that Nell had just had her corns done because she walked much more slowly and it took longer to get to the end of the drive.

'Nell,' said Layla as they passed the hen house, 'does Miss Amelie have many visitors?'

'No, I don't think so. There's a nurse who comes sometimes . . .'

'No, I mean real visitors, like you and Griff and me.'

'I think we're her only regular visitors. Why?'

'It's just . . . she showed Griffin and me a picture of someone and she said he was coming to her house. She said she promised him she'd wait.'

'Did she tell you who he was?'

'She called him John William and she said that he's her sweetheart.'

80

Already they had reached the gate. Nell sighed and leant her elbows on the fence post and her chin in her hands as though the walk had been too much for her. But when she began to speak, Layla knew that it was her heart that ached, not her feet.

'John was Miss Amelie's sweetheart,' she said. 'He was a soldier. He went away to war, a long, long time ago and he didn't come home.'

'Is he dead?' Griffin asked. But Layla didn't need to hear what Nell said to know the answer. That was why she'd had the feeling that something wasn't right. Nell took her elbows off the post then and sat down amongst the tussocky blue grass beside the twin gravel tracks. Layla and Griffin sat down beside her and Blue put his head on her lap.

'Most old people forget some things,' said Nell, stroking Blue's ragged ears. 'It's just part of growing old. But Miss Amelie's forgetfulness is an illness and so far no one's been able to find a cure for it.'

'So she won't get better?' asked Layla.

'No, I'm afraid not. And it's possible she might

get worse. If she does, she might have to go and live in some place where she can be looked after all the time.'

'But Miss Amelie can tell you everything about griffins and gargoyles in architecture,' said Layla, 'and she remembers John William's name and how he used to call her his Queen of Hearts and heaps of other things about him, so how come she doesn't remember that he's . . . dead?'

'I really don't know,' said Nell.

'Was it only when she got old that she forgot John William was dead?' asked Griffin.

'I suppose so,' said Nell. 'I'm just like you, I don't understand it. Nobody really does. But I sometimes wonder if it might be because she's never said goodbye.'

'What do you mean?' asked Layla.

'Some of the soldiers who died were never found. Miss Amelie's John was one of them,' said Nell.

'So she didn't have a funeral for him?' asked Layla slowly.

'Probably not, not like the ones I've told you about anyway.'

Layla thought about her nana dying and of not being allowed to go and say goodbye and of having to be brave all the time.

'And no golden syrup dumplings,' she said, so quietly that Griffin knew she was only talking to herself. The sky had darkened to the colour of violets and Layla thought of Miss Amelie, waiting, always waiting for her soldier boy. All those years she had waited and all for nothing. Layla suddenly felt very angry. 'Then we mustn't tell her,' she shouted. 'It's too late now. We mustn't ever tell her that John William won't come home! Not ever!'

Blue saw Layla's distress. He moved his head, left a warm patch on the old one's lap for her and watched the comforting begin. He knew the girl was in safe hands. The old one had a kind heart. She had rescued him at birth; unwanted, deaf and the runt of a large litter, and had treated him like one of her own ever since. And his boy was a fine boy, an uncommon sort of boy. He too had loved him from the beginning. It was no surprise to Blue when Griffin put his arms around Layla.

'She won't hear it from me,' whispered Griffin, 'cross my heart.'

'Or from me,' said Nell.

And then the stars came out.

A distant sound broke the silence; a comforting sound, the sound of something that Layla knew. It was the Bedford starting up.

'Here comes Ben,' said Nell. 'He'll take you home. It's getting too dark to walk now.' Nell smoothed Layla's hair and dried her face on a corner of her apron. 'I'll meet you tomorrow after school and we'll all go to Miss Amelie's together, to remind her about Senior Citizens' Day.'

9. A Small Miracle

Miss Amelie felt safe in her home, where nothing changed, where she could look at her photographs and think about John William. It would not be easy for her to leave it, even for a few hours.

Because Layla knew this, she gathered all her determination in case it was needed to persuade Miss Amelie. But when she went with Griffin and

Nell to Miss Amelie's house the day before Senior Citizens' Day, Layla was pleasantly surprised.

Miss Amelie had been waiting at the gate for John William again. But when they told her that they hadn't seen him, she let Nell open her silver-frosted gate and take her inside and she didn't seem at all muddled. She did have her tartan trousers on inside out, but that was a mistake anyone could have made. Layla had done it once when she was in a hurry to go tadpoling with Griffin. Miss Amelie had even noticed Nell's lambswool slippers and enquired about her corns.

Nell took the opportunity to sit down on

Miss Amelie's sofa and take off her slippers. It was not often, she said, that people other than Layla showed any interest in her corns. Layla thought she saw a look of longing in Miss Amelie's eyes when she saw the hearts on Nell's toenails, so she reached into her bag and took out her nail polish and the sheet of stickers she had brought with her, just in case.

Miss Amelie didn't want to put her sensible shoes back on after Layla had finished. She just stared and stared at her feet. That was a good sign, Layla thought, so she reminded Miss Amelie.

'It's Seniors' Day tomorrow,' she said.

'Seniors' Day.' Miss Amelie tried the words out, the way she did when she was trying to remember if she'd heard them before. Layla let a few moments go by before she added, 'At St Benedict's, remember?'

'Yes, it's Seniors' Day,' Miss Amelie said. But just to be sure, Nell wrote a note and put it next to Miss Amelie's alarm clock so that she'd remember again in the morning. Layla felt certain that she would; even if she forgot to look at the note, she couldn't help but see her toenails when she put on her shoes.

Tuesday morning was a morning to be remembered, one to be shouted from the hilltops; a morn-ing, as Ben Silk would have said, when memories would be made. Layla knew it straight away. Frost sparkled on the ground, shallow puddles were iced over like magic mirrors and fallen leaves seemed sugar coated. But even so, who could have known that it would be the morning of a small miracle?

'Aren't you cold, Layla?' asked Nell when she and Griffin met Layla on the corner of Chapel Street.

Layla had goose pimples, but she said, 'Just a bit. I've got a jumper in my bag.' But she didn't want to put it on. Not yet, not until Miss Amelie had seen what she was wearing.

Miss Amelie was waiting at the gate again. Layla was pleased that she had got up early. They would have plenty of time to get to school. But as they drew closer she saw that Miss Amelie had her nightie on, and that feeling that all was not well crept over her. Nell started to run, her slippers slapping up and down on the icy pavement.

Miss Amelie clung to the gate as stiff as an icicle. Her hands seemed frozen to the gate. 'Come inside, Amelie, and I'll make us a nice cup of tea,' said Nell firmly. But although Nell coaxed and cajoled, Miss Amelie didn't even seem to hear what she was saying. For an instant, Layla wondered if they should tell the truth about John William, but she knew that Miss Amelie wouldn't understand, that it would only make things worse. So instead she said the only other thing she could think of to get Miss Amelie away from her gate.

'It's okay, Miss Amelie,' she said. 'The train doesn't come until later.' For the first time since her friends had arrived, Miss Amelie noticed them, and it seemed as though the sun had got to her and had begun to thaw her out. Her limbs relaxed and she let Nell untangle her fingers from the wire diamonds on the gate and take her inside.

Nell switched on the electric blanket and made Miss Amelie get straight into bed.

'Stay there while I make you a warm drink, Amelie,' said Nell.

Miss Amelie looked tired, as though she had been waiting for a long time. Her eyes closed and Layla sat down on the edge of her bed with Griffin. In the distance she heard Nell talking softly to someone on the telephone.

'Griff,' whispered Layla, 'I don't think I want to be determined any more.'

'Why not?' asked Griffin, and he noticed that Layla's forget-me-not blue eyes were all watery.

'It's hard to be determined all the time,' she said, 'and besides, I don't think you can rescue someone unless they want to be rescued.'

'You mean Miss Amelie?'

Layla nodded.

'I wanted to take her to school. I thought she'd like it.' She knew that Griffin had put his arm around her shoulders to comfort her, but it made her want to cry more than ever. She had to use the last scrap of her determination to hold her tears back while she confessed to him the other reason, the selfish reason for wanting Miss Amelie to come to school with her. She said, 'I just wanted to have someone special of my own.'

Nell had come to the bedroom door to check on Miss Amelie and to tell them that the doctor was on his way. She heard what Layla said and then she saw what happened before her very eyes.

Miss Amelie sat up in bed as though she had just woken from a good night's sleep. She read the note near her alarm clock. Then she put her feet on the floor and stared at them for a few moments before she said, 'I'm going to school today.'

To some people, this might have seemed a small thing, but Nell said, 'It's a miracle! Small or not, a miracle is still a miracle.'

When the doctor came and examined Miss Amelie and pronounced her fit for school, Layla could feel happiness surging inside her and she had to let it out.

'It's a miracle!' she told the doctor. He smiled, but his eyes still looked sad and she felt sorry for him. Miss Amelie had been out half the night in the freezing cold, yet she wasn't ill and she still remembered it was Seniors' Day. How could he not believe in miracles?

When she asked Nell about it after the doctor had gone, Nell said, 'Some people don't understand that there are things science and technology can't explain. Miracles are one of them and love is another. If it hadn't been for love, Miss Amelie's miracle might not have happened.'

Layla wasn't sure if Nell meant that it was because she loved Miss Amelie or because Miss Amelie loved her that the miracle had happened. But it didn't really matter, she told herself, it was the miracle itself that counted.

10. Queen of Hearts

Nell telephoned for a taxi. It was yellow. This was a good omen, Layla thought, because yellow always reminded her of the sun and the sun made her feel happy. The driver took them all the way up to the front door of St Benedict's as though they were Very Important Persons, which Nell said they were, and they were only a few minutes late.

Miss Beaumont and Mrs Wyman had combined

their classes for the day and were sharing the assembly hall. Layla hadn't thought about how Miss Amelie might feel being amongst so many people she didn't know. But she and Nell stayed close and there was only one awkward moment. That was when Mrs Wyman invited the Seniors to introduce themselves and to talk about why they had come to school.

Miss Amelie listened to the other Seniors, but she didn't introduce herself. So after a while, Layla stood up and said, 'Mrs Wyman, Miss Beaumont, Seniors and girls and boys, this is Miss Amelie.'

Then Miss Amelie stood up. 'Yes, I'm Miss Amelie and I've come to school because . . .'

The silence seemed to go on forever while Miss Amelie stared at all the people in front of her. Then she turned to Layla and studied her eyes, her face, her hair, her clothes and everything about her. At last her eyebrows disappeared up under her neat, silver fringe and Layla knew that she'd remembered why she had come. 'I've come to school,' Miss Amelie said, 'because Layla is my Queen of Hearts.'

Layla thought that she would burst with happiness.

After that everything went smoothly. Mrs Wyman had arranged a foot-painting session. There were troughs of paint; red and blue and yellow, and huge sheets of clean white paper on the floor to walk on.

'Do you want to have a go, Miss Amelie?' Layla asked. Then, because she could still remember her own first day at school when everything had seemed exciting and frightening at the same time, she said, 'I'll come with you if you like.'

Layla took her pink trainers off. Then she and Griffin untied the laces of Miss Amelie's shoes and peeled off her short, white socks. Layla noticed some of the other Seniors looking enviously at Miss Amelie's painted toenails.

Nell couldn't take part because of her corns, but she said, 'Griffin and I are going to help with the morning tea, Amelie, but Layla will take care of you.'

Layla took Miss Amelie's hand and they stepped into the blue paint. It oozed up between their

toes and they laughed. Then they walked across
the paper together, leaving two sets of footprints
behind.

Miss Amelie enjoyed the foot painting so
much that when they had finished, Layla led her
to an easel and gave her a paintbrush and a palette
of rainbow colours. Miss Amelie painted a picture
of a girl in a dress with red hearts on it.

'It's to help me remember,' she told Layla.

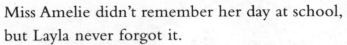

Miss Amelie didn't remember her day at school, but Layla never forgot it.

Two months after Senior Citizens' Day, Miss Amelie went to the station by herself to meet the 9:50pm express. The railway people didn't know about John William. They didn't know that Miss Amelie got muddled either, and they tried to set things straight. They told her that John William wasn't on the train and that the 9:50pm express was the last train that day. It was when Miss Amelie said she'd wait, that they knew something wasn't quite right. That was when they telephoned Katie Wilson's daddy, who was a policeman.

In small towns like Cameron's Creek, policemen know exactly what to do in any emergency. When Mr Wilson arrived at the station he had Nell and Layla and Griffin in his police car.

Later that night, the doctor who didn't believe in miracles came to see Miss Amelie. While he

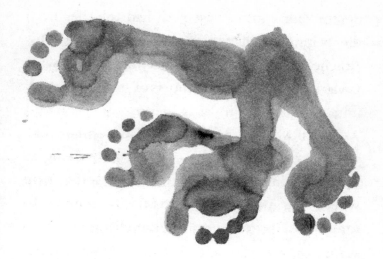

listened to her heart, he looked at the paintings on her bedroom wall; the portrait of Layla and the one of the matching blue footprints. Miss Amelie couldn't remember why they were there, but Nell told the doctor that they were proof of a miracle.

'Perhaps you're right,' the doctor said thoughtfully. Layla was sure that there was a certain wishfulness in his eyes. 'But even if miracles do happen,' he said, 'I don't think we can hope for more than one in a lifetime.'

Layla knew that this was a secret way of saying that Miss Amelie wouldn't get better. The

99

doctor didn't know that Nell had told her from the beginning that there was no cure for Miss Amelie's illness. And he didn't understand what Layla knew: that the memory of even one small miracle is enough to last a lifetime.

And now Miss Amelie was going somewhere safe, somewhere that she couldn't go walking to the station in the middle of the night, somewhere where the people were especially trained to understand forgetfulness and muddledness.

11. Putting Miss Amelie to Rest

The people who looked after Miss Amelie at Lily Lodge were very kind. They understood there were some things that people like Miss Amelie could never remember and some that they could never forget. And like Layla, Griffin and Nell, they were good at keeping secrets, although sometimes their hearts ached to tell.

They hung the painting of the girl in the

heart-patterned dress and the one of the matching blue footprints on her new bedroom wall. Nell had brought an armful of pussy willow down from the Kingdom of Silk. She put it in the tall china vase that had come from Miss Amelie's house in Chapel Street and Layla leant the photographs of herself and Griffin against it. But the fences were very high at Lily Lodge and there was no silver-frosted gate for Miss Amelie to lean on while she waited for John William. And it worried her that he might come and not know where to find her.

Nell said that sometimes when a person died it was a blessing in disguise. On the last Thursday in September, when the violets were blooming and the morning was as misty as a nana's scarf, Miss Amelie stopped waiting for John William. Layla understood then what Nell had meant.

All the people who cared came to St Benedict's church on the day that Miss Amelie was laid to rest. Many wore dark-coloured clothes that matched their sadness, but Layla wore a warm, red velvet jacket and underneath it her Queen of Hearts dress. Mrs Elliott had let the hem down especially because Layla had explained to her how important it was that she wore that dress, the dress that her nana had made. Even though she was sad, she wanted to remember the good things she had shared with Miss Amelie, and with Nana. At the front of the church near the preacher was a beautiful shiny casket covered in scarlet poppies and shafts of coloured light from the windows. When Layla asked if Miss Amelie was inside it, her mother said, 'Shh.' But Nell nodded and squeezed her hand.

The preacher told the story of Miss Amelie from when she had been a little girl until she grew up; how she had learned to be a schoolteacher and had travelled the world looking at griffins and gargoyles. He even talked about John William who, he said, was a very important part of Miss Amelie's story. When everyone stood up and began to sing a song that Layla didn't know, she looked at the coloured windows because she didn't want to think about Miss Amelie being in the casket. On one of the windows was a white bird, its glassy wings outstretched in flight. It reminded Layla of what Katie Wilson had told her, so she imagined Miss Amelie's soul soaring above her in the pitched wooden ceiling of the church and was glad when they opened the doors so it could fly free.

St Benedict's was only two streets away from the cemetery, so only Miss Amelie was driven there. Everyone else walked slowly along behind the gleaming black car. Layla thought how pleased Miss Amelie would have been with the shiny car and the casket because she had been such a neat sort of person. Except for the few times she'd put her trousers on inside out and the day she did the foot painting at school.

At the cemetery, Layla put a posy of violets on the casket. And while the preacher said a prayer she looked up into the sky and said goodbye to Miss Amelie and imagined her soul drifting clear away on the breeze before the casket was lowered into the ground.

After Miss Amelie had been laid to rest, the preacher invited everyone to St Benedict's Hall for the sharing. It was just as Nell had said it would be. No one minded that Layla wasn't brave and that her chin wobbled when she told them about the small miracle, about the portrait Miss Amelie had painted and the matching blue footprints, about being Queen of Hearts for a day.

When Layla was too tired to talk any more, she and Griffin went and sat on the step at the back of the hall and ate corned beef-and-pickle sandwiches with the crusts cut off and pink jelly-cakes, followed by one of Nell's special funeral lamingtons.

The day passed, as all days must, and evening came. Those who cared, who had gathered and shared, returned to their homes. Layla took a long time to eat her chicken stir-fry. Then she sat a while. She had the feeling that there was room inside her for something else, something sweet and sticky.

Her daddy saw the look of wishfulness on her face and said, 'Come here, chicken.' That was when something unexpected and altogether wonderful happened. Mrs Elliott stopped loading the dishwasher when she was only halfway through. She sat down on the couch, because there wasn't enough room on the philosophising chair for three, and patted the seat beside her.

That night, before she went to sleep, Layla Elliott invented a philosophy all of her own. She decided that a tender moment on her mother's lap was probably as good as golden syrup dumplings for the soul.

Golden Syrup Dumplings

Dear Reader,

Ever since I wrote golden syrup dumplings into Layla and Griffin's story, I've had a hankering to eat some. My mum used to make them when I was little and I still love them. So I found this recipe and thought you and your parents might like to try it out too.

Glenda Millard

The Sauce
   30g butter
   $3/4$ cup brown sugar, firmly packed
   $1/2$ cup golden syrup
   1 $2/3$ cups water
   1 teaspoon of lemon rind
   Juice of one lemon
Combine all the above ingredients in a saucepan
and stir over heat without boiling until sugar is
dissolved. Then bring to boil without stirring and
reduce to a simmer.

The Dumplings
   1 $1/4$ cups self-raising flour
   30g butter
   $1/3$ cup golden syrup
   $1/3$ cup milk
Sift flour, rub in butter and gradually stir in golden
syrup and milk. Carefully drop tablespoonfuls of
mixture into simmering sauce. Cover, and simmer
for about 20 minutes. Pierce with a skewer to
see if cooked through. Serve with the sauce and
cream or ice-cream.

About the Author

Glenda Millard was born in the Goldfields region of Central Victoria, Australia and has lived in the area all her life. The communities she has lived in and the surrounding landscapes have provided a rich source of inspiration and settings for many of her stories.

It was not until Glenda's four children became teenagers that she began to write in her spare time. She is now a full-time writer.

Apart from writing, some of Glenda's favourite things are Jack Russell Terriers, hot-air ballooning, eating pizza cooked in the wood-fired oven that her husband built in the backyard and reading books which either make her laugh or cry.

Glenda has published twelve picture books, seven fiction titles for younger readers and three young adult novels. *Layla Queen of Hearts* won the Queensland Premier's Literary Awards 2007 and was shortlisted for the Children's Book Council of Australia Awards.

About the Illustrator

Stephen Michael King has worked as a children's library assistant, animator, designer and illustrator. He has collaborated with authors as varied as Margaret Wild, Jackie French and Tim Winton.

His designs range from children's magazines to farmyard puppet characters for the television show *Bananas in Pyjamas*. He also wrote and illustrated *The Man Who Loved Boxes*, which was shortlisted for the Crichton Award for Children's Book Illustration in 1996. Since then he's authored a further five books (*Patricia, Henry and Amy, Emily Loves to Bounce, Milli, Jack and the Dancing Cat* and *Mutt Dog!*) and is published throughout the world. Stephen has been nominated seven times in the CBCA Awards and selected for America's pick of the list.

Stephen lives on a coastal island in Australia in a mud brick house, surrounded by orchards and forest. He shares this with his wife, two children, their dogs (Muttley and Millie), a couple of guinea pigs, a scaly lorikeet named Sprinkles and the odd visiting cow from their neighbour's place.

Coming soon

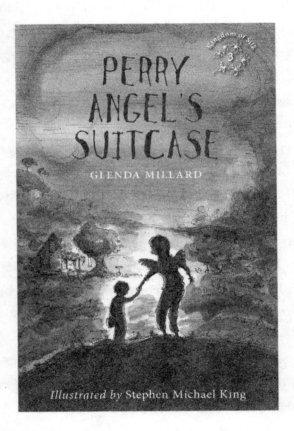